Phantom Drive Sports Cars

by Debbie Dadey
and
Marcia Thornton Jones

illustrated by John Steven Gurney

A
LITTLE APPLE
PAPERBACK

SCHOLASTIC INC.
New York   Toronto   London   Auckland   Sydney

For my new nephew,
Adam Alexander Dadey
—DD

To Hannah Grace Rosenfeld
—MTJ

ISBN 0-590-18982-4

12 11 10 9 8 7 6 5 4 3 2 1   8 9/9 0 1/0 2/0 3/0

Printed in the U.S.A.   40

First Scholastic printing, September 1998

Contents

1

The Opera

"This is horrible," Eddie complained as his whole class avoided the puddles on Smith Avenue and headed toward the Bailey City Opera House. Eddie walked with his friends Howie, Melody, and Liza.

Liza shrugged. "It's not so bad. It's only raining a little bit."

"Rain is only half the problem," Eddie said, pulling his baseball hat over his red hair. "Going to an opera is enough to ruin any day. Why does the third grade have to go to the opera every year?"

"The teachers think it's good for us," Melody explained.

"This year's opera might be kind of neat," Howie told his friends.

Eddie frowned at Howie. "Going to a

1

soccer game would be neat," Eddie said. "This is going to be boring."

Howie pointed to the opera house. "The opera we're going to see is one of the most famous of all time."

Melody smiled and shook rain out of her black pigtails. "It's just the kind of story you'd like. It's full of murder and mystery."

"And beautiful singing," Liza added. She twirled her pink umbrella around and hummed a tune.

"The part about murder sounds okay," Eddie admitted. "But why did they have to add singing? I've heard the singing is really weird. Like this . . ." Eddie jumped in front of his friends and yelled at the top of his voice, "AHHHHAHHHHAH-AHHH!"

Liza shuddered. "If the opera singers sound like that, we're in big trouble."

"If the opera singers sound like that, every dog for miles around will start howling," Melody said with a giggle.

Eddie folded his arms over his chest and continued walking toward the opera house. Their teacher, Mrs. Jeepers, and the rest of their third-grade class were in front of them. Luckily, a girl named Carey was busy telling Mrs. Jeepers about her big new house.

Eddie was glad Mrs. Jeepers hadn't heard his crazy singing. Mrs. Jeepers didn't put up with any mischief from her students. Most kids believed the glowing green brooch she always wore had special magic that made kids like Eddie behave. Some of the third-graders even thought Mrs. Jeepers was a vampire or some kind of monster. A monster that made them go to the opera.

Since Mrs. Jeepers wasn't looking, Eddie jumped right in the middle of a big puddle. Liza, Melody, and Howie hopped out of the way just in time to avoid being splashed. Another kid named Huey wasn't so fast. He turned around and

gave Eddie a dirty look before wiping mud off his raincoat.

"I would rather take a spelling test than go to an opera," Eddie said sadly.

Howie patted Eddie on the back. "It won't be as bad as you think."

Eddie groaned. "It will probably be worse." But then Eddie saw something up ahead of him that made him change his mind.

2

Lamborghini

"It is so cool," Eddie gasped. He was still panting from running down the sidewalk.

Mrs. Jeepers hadn't seen Eddie running. She had turned off the sidewalk and led the rest of the class up the steps to the opera house. She was busy talking to a lady from the ticket office.

"I've never seen anything like it," Melody admitted after checking to make sure Mrs. Jeepers wasn't watching.

"What is it?" Liza asked. The four friends looked at the fancy red sports car parked in front of the opera house.

"It's a Lamborghini Diablo," Howie explained, "one of the neatest sports cars ever made."

"I've never seen one in real life," Eddie admitted, "but I always hoped I would."

Liza shook her head, then pushed blond hair out of her face. "Whatever it is, I don't think it's worth getting killed for. Eddie ran down the sidewalk like a crazy person."

Eddie looked at Liza as if she were the crazy person. "Don't you know anything about cars?" he asked.

"No," Liza said. "What's the big deal? It's just a car."

Eddie held his chest and gasped. "Just a car! Was Mickey Mantle just a baseball player? Was Elvis just a singer?"

Liza's face turned as red as the car. "Elvis was the King of Rock and Roll. He wasn't just a singer."

Howie nodded. "And this is definitely no ordinary car." The rest of the third-graders had noticed the car, too. They stood on the opera house steps, staring at the small windows and sleek, pointed nose of the shiny Lamborghini. Only Howie, Liza, Melody, and Eddie inched closer to the car. Suddenly the door to the car lifted up like the hatch of a space-ship and loud opera music blasted from inside. Liza, Howie, Melody, and Eddie scrambled away from the car and into the shadows of the opera house.

"Is it an alien?" Liza whispered as a tall, thin creature emerged from the depths of the car.

Melody shook her head. "He's a violin-ist." She pointed to the old battered violin case the tall man carried.

The man wore a long, flowing raincoat that he held over his face. He rushed past the kids and into the opera house, almost knocking Liza over.

"What a rude man," Melody complained. "He ought to be ashamed of himself."

"It's okay," Liza told Melody. "He probably didn't mean to bump into me. He was just in a hurry."

"Who cares?" Eddie said. "He left his car open. I'm looking inside!"

3

Erik Gaston

"Rats," Eddie complained as the door to the sports car automatically closed. "I wanted to sit inside."

"That's not your car," Liza told Eddie. "It wouldn't be right to sit in it."

"What I saw inside that car wasn't right, either," Eddie said.

"What are you talking about?" Melody asked Eddie.

Eddie didn't get a chance to explain because their teacher swooped down upon them. "Children, it is time to enter the building," Mrs. Jeepers said. "Please be on your best behavior." Mrs. Jeepers looked right at Eddie when she talked about behaving. Eddie was not known for having the best manners.

Eddie smiled sweetly at Mrs. Jeepers

and followed his friends to their seats. The opera house was an old building with fancy gold decorations all over the walls. Each seat had a fluffy cushion covered with red velvet.

"These are great seats," Howie said. "We're right behind the orchestra pit." He pointed to the musicians who were busy tuning their instruments.

"These are great seats," Eddie agreed, "because they're far away from Mrs. Jeepers." He pointed to Mrs. Jeepers and most of the other third-graders as they found their seats on the far side of the opera house.

"You better not cause any trouble," Melody warned. "Mrs. Jeepers can see us."

"No, she can't," Eddie said with a grin. "There are too many people between us."

"But," Howie said, pointing to the pit, "all the musicians in the pit can see us."

"There's the man who was driving that fancy car," Liza said. The four kids looked at the violinist, but they were only able to see half his face because of the way he was sitting.

"I wish he'd take me for a ride in his Lamborghini," Eddie said. "I wish I were anywhere but here in this horrible place."

Melody noticed that the violinist scowled when Eddie complained. "Shhh," she told Eddie. "I think that man heard you."

"I don't care if the King of England heard me," Eddie muttered. "All this clanging and banging is driving me nuts."

"They're just tuning up," Howie said, listening to the strange sounds coming from the orchestra pit. "The opera will start soon."

"Yippee," Eddie said sarcastically.

Liza had been looking at the program. She pointed to the list of musicians. "That man is Erik Gaston," she said.

"Whoop-de-do," Eddie said. He started to complain more, but the curtain rose and people started singing. Eddie actually enjoyed the story. He liked the idea of a ghost playing pranks on screaming singers. He didn't want his friends to think he liked opera, so when the curtain went down for the intermission Eddie started to complain again.

"How much longer do we have to sit here?" Eddie whined. Melody noticed that Erik Gaston scowled at Eddie's words.

"I could sit here all day," Liza said wistfully. "The opera house is beautiful and the music is pretty."

Eddie rolled his eyes. "I think I'm going to throw up. Why can't Mrs. Jeepers take us to something fun like a hockey game?"

"Opera is cultural," Howie explained. "It's good for you."

"Popcorn and a soda would be good

right now," Eddie said. "I wonder if they have anything to eat out in the lobby."

The four kids headed toward the lobby. Melody looked at the orchestra pit before leaving. Erik Gaston still sat in the pit with only half his face toward the kids. Melody glanced away for just a split second. When she looked back, Erik Gaston was gone.

Melody gasped. "Where did he go?" she asked.

"Eddie's right there," Liza said, pointing in front of her as the four kids squeezed out into the lobby.

"I wasn't talking about Eddie or Howie," Melody said.

Liza slipped around a big lady standing in the doorway. Melody followed her. "Who were you talking about?" Liza asked Melody.

"Never mind," Melody said. "You go on without me. I'll wait here." Melody leaned against a column while her friends went in search of sodas. Melody gulped when a cold hand squeezed her shoulder.

"Tell your friend not to be rude at the opera," a voice said in Melody's ear. "Or he'll be sorry."

4

Phantom

Melody was silent during the rest of the opera. Instead of watching the actors, she kept her eyes glued on the violin player and Eddie.

Every time a singer hit a high note, Eddie put his fingers in his ears. When the masked singer kidnapped the pretty singer, Eddie cupped his hands around his mouth and pretended to boo. The only time Eddie seemed to really listen was when the pretty girl sang her songs.

Thankfully, Mrs. Jeepers was too far away to see Eddie, but somebody else was noticing Eddie's behavior. Even though Melody only saw half of Erik Gaston's face, she knew his mouth was turned down in a frown. Melody thought the violin player looked downright mad.

The longer she watched him, the more worried Melody became.

"What is wrong with you?" Liza whispered. "Are you sick?"

Melody shook her head.

Just then, Eddie stuck out his tongue at the singing monster on the stage. When he did, Erik hit a wrong note on his violin and an ugly squeal filled the auditorium. Several people gasped, but not Eddie. He laughed out loud.

"That violin player sounds like a sick warthog," Eddie said.

"Shhh," Melody hissed. But Eddie didn't pay attention. He snorted and squealed while pretending to play a violin.

Howie was getting ready to jab his friend in the side when Eddie's folding chair suddenly collapsed, trapping Eddie between the seat and back. Liza giggled at Eddie's legs and arms sticking out at odd angles.

A funny noise from the orchestra pit

caught Melody's attention. She couldn't believe what she saw. Erik Gaston was looking straight at Eddie, and Erik was laughing!

Eddie was so busy trying to get comfortable in his broken chair that he didn't have time to be rude during the rest of the opera. When the final curtain fell, Eddie didn't clap for any of the singers except one. He stood up and cheered when the pretty singer stepped to the center of the stage. Howie and Liza stared at Eddie, but Melody watched Erik Gaston instead.

What Melody saw made her shiver. Erik Gaston frowned at Eddie. And then, right before Melody's eyes, Erik Gaston disappeared from the orchestra pit.

"You act like you just saw a ghost," Howie whispered when Melody gasped.

"Or a phantom," Eddie said with a laugh.

Melody's eyes got big. She looked at each of her friends. "For once," Melody said, "Eddie is right! Bailey City has a phantom and I just saw him!"

Howie grinned. "Of course you saw a phantom. This entire opera was about a phantom haunting an opera house because he loved a pretty singer. It's a famous story from an old book."

"I'm not talking about pretend phantoms," Melody snapped. "I'm talking about a real phantom. It was that man in the orchestra pit who drove that cool car."

"The only pit where you saw a real phantom is in the black hole of your brain." Eddie laughed.

Liza patted Melody's shoulder. "The boys are right," she told her friend. "Phantoms are made-up ghosts."

"And they don't drive sports cars," Howie added.

"But I saw him!" Melody argued. "He disappeared before my very eyes."

"The only thing disappearing from this place is our class," Howie pointed out. "And if we don't hurry, we'll be left behind!"

Howie was right. Mrs. Jeepers was leading the long line of third-graders down the aisle toward the door. Howie and Liza hurried after them. Melody followed Eddie.

As they left their seats, a huge piece of scenery fell off the stage. It landed right on Eddie's broken chair.

5
Wrong

Melody screamed and grabbed Eddie's arm, pulling him away from the fallen piece of scenery. "Did you see that?" she said. "That almost hit Eddie."

"A piece of scenery can't aim for anything," Howie pointed out. "It was an accident."

"Don't be so sure," Melody said. "I watched Erik Gaston during the opera. I don't think he liked how Eddie behaved."

"Grown-ups never like the way Eddie behaves," Liza said. "That makes Erik normal."

"Grown-ups in Bailey City are never normal," Eddie said.

"But not all grown-ups disappear," Melody said. "And they don't cause Eddie's chair to break."

"I wish all grown-ups would disappear," Eddie said with a laugh. "Then we could do whatever we wanted."

"You do what you want anyway," Liza pointed out. "That's why most grown-ups think you're rude."

"AHHHH!" Melody screamed.

Liza jumped and Howie ducked. Eddie turned in circles, ready to karate chop monsters in two.

"Why are you yelling?" Howie asked when he saw they weren't being attacked by a flock of ghosts.

"Liza helped me remember something," Melody said.

"That you're crazy?" Eddie asked.

Melody glared at Eddie before answering. "I just remembered what happened in the lobby when you went to get a drink," Melody explained. "Somebody told me to warn Eddie to stop being rude!"

"That sounds like it could have been

anybody in Bailey City," Howie said matter-of-factly.

"Who was it?" Liza asked.

Melody shrugged. "I didn't see his face, but I think I know who it was," she said seriously.

"WHO?" her three friends asked at once.

"The Phantom of Bailey City," Melody told them. "Erik Gaston!"

Howie laughed as the four friends hurried after the rest of their class. Mrs. Jeepers was already out the door and halfway down the steps when the four friends finally caught up to the group.

"You can't really believe Erik Gaston is the Phantom of Bailey City," Howie told her.

But Melody didn't answer because just then the bright red sports car raced down the street. When it reached the line of third-graders heading toward Bailey Elementary, the sports car slowed down.

Melody got the eerie feeling somebody was staring at her through the dark windows of the car before it sped up again and disappeared from sight.

"Wasn't that Erik Gaston's car?" Liza asked.

Melody nodded. "It's the phantom's car," she said with a trembling voice.

Eddie laughed. "Erik can't be a phantom," he told his friend. "Remember, phantoms don't drive sports cars! They haunt houses and play tricks on people they don't like."

"People," Melody said, staring straight at Eddie, "that are rude? Erik Gaston doesn't like Eddie because he didn't behave at the opera."

"None of that matters," Howie said as the third-graders got close to their school. "The opera is over and we'll never see Erik Gaston again."

But Howie was wrong.

The third-graders hurried to their classroom, ready to copy math problems from the board. But Mrs. Jeepers stood at the front of the room and spoke in her quiet Transylvanian accent.

"Class," she said, "I have a wonderful surprise."

"Oh, no," Eddie groaned. He was used to his teacher's surprises. They usually meant more work.

Mrs. Jeepers glared at Eddie and gently rubbed the brooch she always wore. Eddie shut his mouth and pretended to listen.

"Two of the performers from the opera are friends of mine," their teacher told them. "I know them from long, long ago. They offered to talk with you about the opera. Please welcome Mr. Erik and Miss Christine."

The rest of the third-graders clapped, but Melody stared in horror when their classroom door swung open and Miss Christine and Mr. Erik swept into the room.

Erik wore his flowing raincoat with the

collar turned up, and a hat that shaded half of his face. He reminded Melody of an evil spy.

Eddie stopped clapping and poked Melody. "She looks just like a princess in a fairy tale," he said, staring at Christine.

It was true. Christine still wore her long frilly dress and white gloves. But that's not what Melody saw. She noticed that Erik stared at Christine for a very long time. In fact, it was almost as if he'd forgotten where he was. He kept staring at the beautiful opera singer until Mrs. Jeepers got his attention by clearing her throat.

Erik turned away from Christine and bowed to Mrs. Jeepers. Then he turned to the class. He spoke in a low voice that sounded very sad.

"Opera," he said, "is my life. The music, the stories, and the costumes all make me believe that anything is possible. It is my hope that each of you will come to appreciate the beauty of opera."

Without saying another word, Erik placed his violin case on Mrs. Jeepers' desk. He flipped up the tarnished brass latches and slowly pulled out his ancient scratched violin. He closed his eyes and played.

The entire class listened to the sad notes pouring from Erik's instrument.

And then, Christine began to sing.

6

Phantom of Bailey School

"That's the saddest thing I ever heard," Liza said with a sigh.

Liza and her friends Melody, Howie, and Eddie stood under the giant oak tree on the playground. They had listened to Erik and Christine right up until recess, but none of them felt like running or kicking a soccer ball.

Howie nodded. "Erik's violin sounded like it was crying over the sad words Christine sang about her lost love."

"I'll tell you what's sad," Eddie mumbled. "Four healthy kids moping over made-up gooey love songs. It's not even raining anymore. We should go play kickball."

"I don't think those were made-up

songs," Melody told him. "I think they were for real."

"What do you mean?" Liza asked.

"Didn't you see the way Erik looked at Christine?" Melody asked. "He's obviously in love with her just like the phantom was in love with the Christine of the opera we just saw. They even have the same names!"

"Big deal," Eddie said. "Adults fall in love all the time. They don't know any better. Besides, Erik might as well give up. A beautiful singer like that would never fall in love with an ugly violin player."

Liza shook her finger in front of Eddie's nose. "What a horrible thing to say," she told him. "Don't you know that looks don't matter? It's what's on the inside that counts!"

"Then Eddie is in big trouble," Howie said with a laugh. "He's rotten inside and out!"

Eddie puffed out his chest. "There's nothing wrong with the way I look."

"But," Melody said, "there is something wrong with the way Erik looks."

"How can you tell?" Liza asked. "We've never gotten a good look at his face."

"That's true," Howie added. "He always has it covered up with his hat or coat."

"Just like the real phantom covered his face," Melody finished.

"There are no such things as real phantoms," Eddie told Melody.

"You don't know that for sure, and if you're wrong, Christine may be in danger," Melody said. "The phantom in the play took the beautiful singer to an awful underground room and locked her up because she didn't love him back. Don't you remember?"

"I remember," Eddie said, "that it was just an opera. That means it's all made-up. Erik is not a real phantom, and I'll prove it."

"How?" Melody asked.

"By becoming," Eddie said with a grin, "the Phantom of Bailey City!"

7

Argh!!!

Liza folded her arms in front of her stomach. "Exactly how are you going to become the Phantom of Bailey City?" she asked.

Eddie shrugged. "Okay, I'll just be a regular kid and prove that Erik is a regular guy, too."

"What are you talking about?" Melody asked.

"I'll trick him," Eddie said.

Howie snapped his fingers. "We'll get him to show his face."

"The Phantom of the Opera never showed his whole face," Liza said.

"Exactly," Howie explained. "If Eddie and I get Erik Gaston to show his face, then we'll prove he's not a phantom."

Liza pointed her finger at Eddie. "Do you promise not to be mean to Mr. Gaston?"

Eddie smiled. "Me, mean? I'm never mean."

Melody rolled her eyes, then looked at the school building. "There's Erik and Christine now."

Eddie didn't waste a second. As Erik helped Christine down the school steps, Eddie raced over to them. Howie zipped after him.

"You don't think Eddie would embarrass Erik in front of Christine, do you?" Liza asked Melody.

Melody shook her dark head. "There's no telling what Eddie might do. Maybe we'd better go keep an eye on him and Howie."

When Liza and Melody got to the school steps Eddie was standing on his head and screaming opera music. "ARGH-ARGH-ARRRRRRRRRRRRRGH!"

Christine smiled at Eddie. "That's very interesting music you're making," she said.

Eddie jumped up and beamed at Christine. "Thank you," Eddie told her. Erik didn't say a word, or even move his head.

"I bet I can do a flip and sing at the same time," Eddie said, but Christine didn't give him a chance.

She put a hand on Eddie's shoulder and said, "I didn't realize you enjoyed opera quite so much."

Eddie flashed his big white teeth at Christine. "Opera is my life."

Then Howie looked at Erik. He hadn't moved and definitely hadn't shown the rest of his face. "Of course," Howie said loudly, "the reason we love opera so much is due to the beauty of the lead singer."

Christine blushed and patted Howie on the shoulder with her gloved hand. "You boys are much too kind."

Howie noticed that the part of Erik's

41

face that showed was red, too. He didn't look embarrassed, though. He looked mad.

Christine pulled tickets out of her small gold purse. "Since you are such fans of opera, why don't you and a grown-up be my guest for this evening's performance?"

Liza did a little curtsy and accepted the tickets. "That is very nice of you. Thank you."

Erik led Christine away and helped her into his Lamborghini. The kids heard opera music blaring inside as the red car sped away.

8

Jealous

Eddie turned toward Howie. "What's the big idea?" Eddie asked.

"What did I do wrong?" Howie asked.

"You've ruined my whole night," Eddie complained, looking at the five free opera tickets.

Howie shrugged. "I was trying to help you."

Eddie slumped down on the school steps and put his face in his hands. Melody looked at Eddie. "Is he crying?" she whispered.

Eddie looked up. "I should cry. I have a right to cry. Now I have to go to the opera twice in one day. That's more than any human should have to suffer through."

Howie laughed. "Why are you so upset? You're the one who said you wanted to prove Erik Gaston wasn't a phantom. This will give you the chance."

"It will give me the chance to die of boredom," Eddie muttered. "My grandmother wants to go to the opera. I'll give her one of the tickets."

Melody twirled one of her black braids around her finger. "I think the opera is just the place we need to go."

"Are you crazy?" Eddie snapped.

"No," Melody said, "but Erik is crazy about Christine. Didn't you see how jealous Erik got when Howie complimented her?"

"That's right," Liza said. "His face was redder than Eddie's hair."

"And that jealousy gave me a great idea," Melody told her friends.

"What is it?" Liza asked.

Melody raced away from the playground. "I'll tell you tonight at the opera."

That night, just before seven o'clock, Eddie's grandmother parked her dusty green van in front of the Bailey City Opera House, right behind the red Lamborghini. Eddie, Melody, Liza, Howie, and Eddie's grandmother hopped out of the van.

"My," Eddie's grandmother said, pointing to the Lamborghini, "that is a snazzy-looking vehicle."

"The phantom drives that car," Liza blurted without thinking.

"You mean the phantom from the opera?" Eddie's grandmother asked. "The singer who plays his part?"

Liza didn't answer, but Melody whispered to Liza, "We mean the phantom *of* the opera."

As the kids settled into their red velvet seats in the opera house Eddie whispered to Melody, "Okay, we're here. Now what's your plan?"

Melody took a worried look at the orchestra pit, then held up the big shopping bag she had with her. "In this bag," she whispered, "we have everything we need to trap a phantom."

9

Secret Admirer

Eddie took one look in Melody's shopping bag and laughed so loudly somebody three rows behind them said, "Shhh!" Eddie didn't pay any attention. Instead, he reached into Melody's bag and pulled out a huge bundle of orange flowers.

"So your fantastic plan is to trap a phantom with mums?" he asked. "What do you think a phantom is? A giant bumblebee?"

"Wait," Howie said. "I think I know what Melody's planning."

Liza huddled close to her friends and nodded. "If it's true that Erik is the real phantom," Liza whispered, "then he'll get very jealous if he thinks Christine has a secret admirer."

"Exactly," Melody said. "We just need to put these flowers someplace with this note. When Erik sees it, we'll see by his reaction if he's the real phantom."

"The only reaction we'll see is an allergic reaction," Eddie said, sniffing the bundle of flowers in his hands until he sneezed.

Melody handed Eddie a tissue. "Runny noses are the least of our worries," she said. "If Erik really is the phantom, then everybody in this theater is in danger. It's up to us to save them."

Eddie rolled his eyes. "The only thing we have to worry about is your phantom brain that nobody can find. Besides, even if you're right, what harm can a violin-playing phantom do?"

"Don't you remember?" Melody gasped. "In the opera, the phantom made the big glass chandelier fall on the audience because he was mad."

Eddie, Melody, Liza, and Howie all looked at the ceiling over their heads.

Sure enough, there was a giant chandelier hanging right over their heads by a single skinny chain.

Liza gulped. "That chain doesn't look strong enough to hold up all that glass," she whimpered.

"It's safe," Howie said, but he didn't sound very sure, "as long as nobody makes it fall."

"And the only person who can make it fall," Melody said, "is the phantom."

Eddie glanced up at the chandelier before speaking. "I still think this talk of phantoms is dumb," he said. "But I'll go along with your plan. How will you get the flowers to Christine?"

As it turned out, the kids didn't have to figure that out.

Eddie's grandmother glanced at Eddie and smiled. "How nice," she said. "You brought flowers for the lead singer."

Even in the dim light of the opera theater, Liza could see the tips of Eddie's ears turning pink. He quickly tossed the bundle of flowers at Howie. "I didn't bring them," Eddie said. "They belong to Howie."

Eddie's grandmother smiled. "Giving flowers is a traditional way to show you like the star's singing," his grandmother told Howie. "You'll have to hurry if you plan to get them to her dressing room before the show."

"Her dressing room?" Howie stammered.

Eddie's grandmother nodded. "It should be right behind the stage."

Howie stumbled over Liza's and Eddie's feet on his way to the aisle. He made it a point to step on Melody's foot. "This was your idea," he hissed to Melody. "You should be coming with me."

Melody pretended she hadn't heard a word.

Howie made his way backstage to look for Christine's dressing room. It was down a dark, twisting hallway. Finally,

Howie found the door with Christine's name on it. He glanced at the card Melody had scribbled. It said, "From a secret admirer." Howie carefully placed the bouquet of flowers in front of the door.

"I hope nobody sees me," he muttered as he hurried back the way he came.

But somebody was watching.

10

Watch Out!

Howie barely made it back to his seat in time. As he sat down, the theater lights dimmed. The audience waited in silence, but the orchestra in the pit didn't start playing.

"Why are they waiting?" Liza whispered.

Melody pointed to the empty chair. "Erik is missing," she hissed. "They must be waiting for him."

They didn't have to wait long. Erik swept into the pit. He was in such a hurry that his long coat flew up and knocked a music stand down. It landed with a giant crash.

"Smooth move," Eddie blurted out.

"Shhh," Melody warned.

As soon as Erik sat down, he put the

scarred violin to his chin and started to play. The curtain swished up and there stood Christine. When the spotlight hit Christine, Liza gasped.

"Is that what I think it is?" Liza asked.

Melody nodded. "It looks like Christine got the gift from her secret admirer."

The entire audience couldn't help but notice the way Christine had laced the orange mums through her hair like a crown.

As soon as Erik saw the flowers in Christine's hair, he stopped playing in the middle of the song. Very slowly, he turned and stared straight at Howie. The dim theater lights made it impossible to see his face, but Melody could still make out the gleam of his black eyes.

"Watch out!" Eddie blurted out. "He's looking at you!"

"Shhh," Melody warned.

Howie slid down in his seat and tried to hide, but it was no use. Erik stared at Howie for a full music measure. Then he

slowly put the violin back to his chin and played.

"He knows you brought the flowers," Melody whispered. "And it made him mad."

"But," Eddie argued, "you haven't proved anything. As far as we know, Erik liked the flowers."

"Eddie has a point," Liza admitted. "Erik isn't acting like a phantom."

"Then maybe we haven't made him jealous enough!" Melody said.

"What does that mean?" Howie said out loud.

"Shhh," several people hissed from the row behind them.

Melody put her finger to her lips, but that didn't stop her from whispering. "Don't worry," she said. "I have another idea."

11

Chocolate Ants

"We need money," Melody told her friends when the curtain came down for intermission.

Eddie nodded. "I need about a million bucks."

"No," Melody said, pointing toward the lobby. "We need money to buy chocolates."

"Yummy," Liza said. "Chocolate sounds delicious."

"It's not for us to eat," Melody explained. "It's to give to Christine to make Erik jealous."

Howie held up his hand. "I don't know if that's such a good idea. He looked like he wanted to kill me already."

"It doesn't matter anyway," Eddie said,

dumping out his pockets. Out of one came three lint balls, a broken whistle, and a rubber frog. The other pocket held exactly twenty-three cents. "We couldn't buy a chocolate-covered ant with twenty-three cents."

Liza, Melody, and Howie checked their pockets, but they had no money at all. Eddie's grandmother leaned over Eddie. "What are you children up to?" she asked.

"We were going to buy Christine candy," Liza told her truthfully, "but we don't have enough money."

"What a sweet idea," Eddie's grand-mother said. "You children are so thoughtful." She pulled a five-dollar bill out of her purse. "You may use this to buy the star some candy. I hope it will be enough."

Liza smiled. "Thank you. That's very nice of you." The four kids hopped up and rushed out to the lobby.

Eddie came back from the refreshment

counter with a big bag of jelly beans. He held it up for his friends to see.

"Eddie," Melody complained. "You were supposed to buy chocolate. Jelly beans are not very romantic."

"Hey," Eddie snapped. "I got pink jelly beans. They're as romantic as chocolate. This whole thing is stupid anyway. We should just eat these ourselves."

Melody grabbed the bag from Eddie. "I'll hang on to these for safekeeping."

"We'd better hurry if we're going to deliver these to Christine before the opera starts back up," Liza told her friends.

Howie backed away from the jelly beans. "I'm not taking them by myself. That backstage area is creepy."

"Don't be a wimp," Eddie told him. "We'll go with you."

The four kids slipped down the back hallway. The bright lights quickly faded and they found themselves surrounded by shadows. Their footsteps echoed on the wooden floor.

"If I were a phantom this is where I would hang out," Eddie admitted. "Away from the lights of the stage."

Liza gulped. "Let's just deliver these jelly beans as fast as we can. I want to get back to the bright lights."

"There's nothing to get nervous about," Eddie said. "We're the only ones here."

"I'm not so sure about that," Melody said. "I think I hear something." The four kids stopped and listened. A faint click of footsteps echoed behind them.

"Oh, my gosh," Liza squealed. "The phantom is after us."

"We're trapped," Melody whispered. "The phantom is between us and the rest of the world."

12

Lost Forever

"What are we going to do?" Liza asked, backing up against the wall.

Howie looked down the long dark hall toward Christine's dressing room. "Let's hurry to Christine. I bet she can help us." The four kids rushed off in the opposite direction of the footsteps.

"Here it is," Howie said as he stopped in front of the door marked with a star and a small name tag. Eddie pushed Howie aside. "Let me knock," Eddie said. Eddie banged on the door as hard as he could.

But nobody came to the door.

"She better hurry," Melody hissed. "The footsteps are getting closer."

Liza sniffed as if she might cry. "What

are we going to do?" she whimpered. "If we stand here, the phantom will get us."

"Liza's right," Eddie said. "We better get out of here."

Howie grabbed Eddie's arm. "I didn't think you believed in phantoms," Howie said.

"When I'm standing in the middle of a dark hall," Eddie said, "and footsteps are chasing me, then I'll believe in anything!"

"What are we going to do?" Liza asked.

"I'll tell you what we'll do," Eddie said. "We'll get out of here."

"But the phantom is in our way," Melody said.

"No problem," Eddie said. "We'll go the other way!"

When Eddie turned and ran, his three friends hurried after him. They raced down the hallway until they came to a heavy door. Eddie pulled open the door to find a steep flight of stairs. Without stopping to think, Eddie, Howie, Melody, and Liza galloped down the steps.

A maze of old scenery filled the basement. A single bare lightbulb cast crazy shadows across the room.

"Where are we?" Melody asked.

Liza batted away a sticky spiderweb. "This must be where they store all the old scenery," she said.

"Going down the steps was stupid," Melody said. "Now we're trapped."

"Maybe not," Howie said. "There could be another way out on the other side."

Howie led the way across the huge basement, weaving in and out of the piles of wooden scenery. They were halfway across the room when Eddie grabbed Howie's arm.

"Wait," he hissed. "I think I hear something."

Melody and Liza stopped to listen, too. Somewhere, from behind them, came the soft sound of shoes scooting across the floor. "Do you think it's the phantom?" Liza whispered.

Before anybody could answer, a huge wooden horse crashed to the floor.

"RUN!" Melody screamed. She pushed past Howie and raced to the far side of the dingy basement. A single door was hidden behind a pile of old boxes. "Follow me," Melody said.

She pulled open the door and was faced with pitch-black. Somewhere, something dripped, and it smelled sour.

"Sounds like water," Howie said.

"It reminds me," Melody said, "of the lake in the opera about the phantom."

"That's impossible," Eddie said. "There can't be a lake in a basement."

"Nothing," Liza said, "is impossible. After all, we saw water deep under Ruby Mountain when we explored the cave. Who knows, maybe this basement goes right to that cave."

"Liza's right," Melody said. "This is probably how the real phantom escapes

from the Bailey City Opera House when he can't use his sports car."

"Oh, no," Liza said. "We never should have come down here. Nobody even knows we're here. We could get lost forever and nobody would be able to find us."

"Either that," Eddie said, "or the phantom will catch us."

"We should holler for help," Howie said. He opened his mouth to scream, but just then a pale hand reached out from behind a wooden tree to cover Howie's mouth.

13

Who Needs Love?

"Ahhhhhhhh!" Melody screamed. "The phantom got Howie!"

Christine giggled. "I think perhaps you've had a little too much opera for one day. It's just me."

Christine dropped her hand from Howie's mouth and stepped out from behind the painted tree.

"Thank goodness," Melody said. "We thought the jealous Phantom of the Opera was after us."

Christine patted Melody on the shoulder. "That story is only pretend."

"Do you mean you're not afraid of phantoms?" Liza asked.

Christine smiled. "I wouldn't be afraid even if there were a real phantom because I have four brave third-graders

71

here to protect me." Christine reached up and plucked four mums from her flower crown. She handed Howie, Melody, Liza, and Eddie each one of the flowers. "With wonderful fans like you, I don't need anyone else," she added.

Just then, a door slammed on the other end of the basement.

"What was that?" Liza gasped.

But Christine didn't seem bothered. "This old building is full of strange sounds," she said. "Now tell me why you're in the basement."

"We were looking for you," Melody said. She smiled and handed Christine the jelly beans. "We brought you a treat."

"You are so marvelous," Christine said, giving each kid a big hug. Eddie could smell sweet perfume when Christine squeezed him.

"Now," Christine told the kids, "we'd better hurry back. The music is ready to begin."

The kids followed Christine back up

the steps and down the long dark hallway. Howie, Melody, Liza, and Eddie waved to Christine as they left her by the stage.

The theater was quiet as the four kids found their seats. Suddenly, a loud squeal echoed through the theater. "What was that?" Howie asked.

"It sounded like a maniac driving outside the opera house," Eddie told his friends.

"There's only one person around here who would drive like that," Melody said. "The phantom!"

The four kids peered into the orchestra pit. Sure enough, Erik Gaston was missing. "Where did he go?" Liza asked.

They didn't have to wait long to find out. A tall woman wearing a long black dress stepped out from behind the curtain and cleared her throat. "Mr. Erik Gaston had to leave. Please welcome his replacement, Peter Simpson."

The rest of the audience clapped as a

skinny man with a long mustache strode into the orchestra pit.

Liza leaned over Melody. "I bet Erik was so jealous he couldn't take it anymore."

"Do you think it was his car leaving?" Melody said softly.

Liza nodded. "Erik must have heard what Christine said in the basement. He knew she would never love him so he drove away in his fancy red car."

Eddie shrugged. "He was smart. After all, who needs love when they can drive a great sports car?"

"At least we're safe," Melody said, "now that the phantom is gone."

Just then the new violin player sat down in Erik's chair. When he did, the chair cracked, and the tall man fell to the floor. The entire first two rows laughed, but Melody's eyes got big.

"Maybe," she said, "the phantom of the Bailey City Opera isn't gone after all!"